The Pug who wanted to be a Bunny

With special thanks to Anne Marie Ryan.
Illustrations by Nina Jones and Artful Doodlers.

ORCHARD BOOKS

First published in Great Britain in 2020 by The Watts Publishing Group

1 3 5 7 9 10 8 6 4 2

A CIP catalogue record for this book
is available from the British Library.

ISBN 978 1 40836 159 7

Printed and bound in Great Britain by Clays Ltd, Elcograf S.p.A
The paper and board used in this book are made from wood from responsible sources.

Orchard Books
An imprint of
Hachette Children's Group
Part of The Watts Publishing Group Limited
Carmelite House
50 Victoria Embankment
London EC4Y 0DZ

An Hachette UK Company
www.hachette.co.uk
www.hachettechildrens.co.uk

The Pug
who wanted to be a
Bunny
Bella Swift

Contents

Chapter One

Sunlight streamed through the kitchen windows as Peggy the pug's family ate their breakfast. As usual, the little dog sat by Chloe's chair, her big brown eyes gazing up at the curly-haired girl imploringly. Peggy loved every member of her family, but Chloe was her special friend. She was also the most likely to share her breakfast!

Peggy whimpered quietly and wagged her curly tail. Chloe slipped Peggy a piece of bacon under the table and she gobbled it down. *Yum!*

"I saw that," Dad scolded Chloe over the top of his tablet. "You know you're not supposed to feed Peggy from the table."

"Why not?" protested Peggy. Crispy bacon was *soooo* much tastier than dog food! But to her family it just sounded like barking. Humans couldn't understand animal language.

"But you and Mum are always saying

how important it is to share," said Chloe, giving her dad a cheeky grin. "Anyway, I can't help it. Peggy looks so cute."

Chloe's little sister, Ruby, looked down at Peggy and cooed. "Who's the cutest doggie in the whole world? Is it Peggy? Yes, it is!"

Finn, Chloe's older brother, snapped a

close-up of Peggy's face with his phone. "I'm tagging it #pugmug," he said, sharing it on his social media.

Peggy sighed happily. She loved weekends, when all three children were at home.

Dad put down his tablet and smiled. "Good news! The forecast says it's going to be sunny all weekend. I've got a lot to do in the garden. The spring greens are starting to come up, but I want to sow some carrots and runner beans."

"I love springtime," said Chloe. "It's my birthday, and then the Easter Bunny comes!"

"Actually," said Mum, sipping her

coffee, "Easter comes first this year."

"But my birthday was before Easter last year," said Chloe.

"Easter isn't on the same day every year, dummy," said Finn.

"This year your birthday is the week *after* Easter," explained Dad.

"That reminds me," said Mum. "I want to make some hot cross buns for the café, but I was thinking of trying out some exciting flavours." Mum had recently opened a dog-friendly café called Pups and Cups. "Any ideas?"

"Smoky bacon flavoured!" barked Peggy, though of course Mum didn't understand her. The café was good for dogs, so Peggy thought the snacks should be too!

"Unicorn hot cross buns," suggested Ruby.

"Interesting . . ." said Mum.

"You should make spicy ones," said Finn, shaking some hot sauce on his scrambled eggs. Lately, Finn added extra-hot spicy sauce to everything. Chloe had told Peggy that he did it because he thought it made him look tough.

"Gross," said Chloe, wrinkling her nose. "Nobody wants to eat a bun that will make their eyes water. Make triple chocolate ones – with white, milk and dark chocolate. Mmm . . ."

"Those are all great ideas," said Mum. "I'll test them out today."

"I'll help!" Ruby offered eagerly.

"Can I ride my bike to Ellie's house?" asked Chloe. "She invited me and Hannah over yesterday at school. She said she had something exciting to show us."

"That's fine," said Mum. "What do you suppose it is?"

"Ooh! Maybe she's got a unicorn!" said Ruby.

"Yeah, I'm sure it's that," said Finn, rolling his eyes.

"Hannah and I tried to get her to give us a hint," said Chloe, "But she just twitched her nose mysteriously."

"Maybe she was hinting that you smell bad," laughed Finn.

"You're the one who stinks!" said Chloe, giving her brother a shove. "Your feet smell like a cross between mouldy cheese and rotting fish."

"OK, OK, that's enough," said Dad. "I could use some help in the garden today – any volunteers?"

Finn shrugged. "I'll help."

Chloe laughed. "That's going to make you even stinkier!"

Later that morning, Chloe and Peggy went outside to the garage, which was crammed full of bicycles, sledges and storage boxes. There was a workbench with tools hanging from pegs on the wall and a stack of wooden planks next to it.

As Peggy sniffed around the garage, Chloe moved a paddling pool to the side and pulled out a rusty green bike covered with faded dinosaur stickers. Brushing cobwebs off the frame, she

wheeled it out of the garage. She swung her leg over the seat and frowned. "I must have grown over the winter."

Chloe tried to pedal the bike forward, but it barely moved. The front tyre was as flat as Peggy's nose!

Chloe got off the bike and sighed. "It's got a puncture."

Peggy trotted behind Chloe as she went through the gate into the back garden. Spring flowers, like lemon-yellow daffodils and bright purple crocuses, painted the flowerbeds with colour. At the end of the garden was Dad's pride and joy – the vegetable patch. Green shoots, carefully labelled with white

sticks, sprouted from neat rows of soil.

"Dad," called Chloe, going over to where Dad and Finn were working, "my bike has a flat tyre. Can you mend it?"

"Sorry, honey," said Dad, resting on the handle of his spade. Sweat beaded his forehead. "I can't right now. I'll need to pick up an inner tube at the cycle shop."

"Never mind," grumbled Chloe. "It's too small for me now. I hate that ugly old bike anyway."

"Hey," said Finn, flicking a worm at his sister. "That used to be my bike."

"Exactly," said Chloe.

Chloe and Peggy headed inside. Peggy sniffed – something smelled good! The kitchen counter was covered in baking ingredients. As Mum stirred something in a bowl, Ruby tipped rainbow-coloured sprinkles into the mixture.

"We're making unicorn hot cross buns!" cried Ruby, a smudge of flour on her nose.

"My bike has a flat tyre. Can you drive me to Ellie's house, Mum?" asked Chloe.

"I've just put the first batch of buns in the oven," said Mum. "It's a lovely day – why don't you just walk?"

Good idea! thought Peggy, going over to her lead and wagging her tail.

"Peggy wants to go too," said Ruby, pointing.

"I'm going to be so late!" sighed Chloe, clipping on Peggy's lead.

As they walked to Ellie's house, Peggy breathed in the scents of springtime – damp soil, freshly cut grass and fragrant pink apple blossom. Barbecue smoke wafted from one of the houses they

passed. The sound of music drifted from the back garden, where a party was happening.

"I wonder if Mum and Dad will let me have a birthday party," Chloe said to Peggy. "Maybe I could have a swimming party, like Hannah had. Or a pizza-making party like Ellie's."

Chloe turned up the front path to Ellie's house and her friend flung the door open. "I thought you'd never get here!" Ellie crouched down and patted Peggy on the head. "Hi, Pegs."

"Sorry I'm late," said Chloe, unclipping Peggy's lead. "I had to walk because Mum and Dad were busy with my brother and sister. You're lucky to be an only child."

Ellie shrugged. "It gets lonely sometimes. I wish I had a sister."

"Well, you can borrow mine any time you want," said Chloe. "So what's your big news?"

"Come on," said Ellie, taking her

friend's hand. "I'll show you."

They went outside. At the end of the patio was a wooden rabbit hutch where Daisy, Ellie's pet rabbit, lived.

Peggy pressed her nose against the wire mesh to peer inside.

"Oh my goodness!" gasped Chloe.

Snuggled up next to Daisy were five tiny baby bunnies!

Chapter Two

"They are soooo cute," said Chloe, staring at the baby rabbits, her eyes wide.

Two of the bunnies were white, two were black, and the smallest one had black and white patches like her mum. The other babies were fast asleep, nestled against their mother's side, but the littlest

bunny's bright blue eyes stared at Chloe and Peggy. She hopped over to the mesh window and sniffed them curiously with her tiny pink nose.

"Congratulations, Daisy!" barked Peggy. "Your babies are beautiful."

"Thank you," the rabbit replied, gazing proudly at her brood. Then she yawned.

"I love them, but looking after so many babies is hard work."

"Can I hold them?" Chloe asked Ellie.

Ellie shook her head. "Not yet. The vet said we need to wait until they're a bit older to hold them. Baby bunnies need peace and quiet." She grinned. "It's been hard keeping it a secret."

The doorbell rang and the little bunny's long ears twitched.

Ellie ran inside to answer the door. A moment later she returned with a girl holding a little brown terrier in a sparkly pink coat.

"Hi, Hannah!" said Chloe.

"Hi, Princess!" barked Peggy.

Hannah put Princess down and she ran over to Peggy, her tail wagging excitedly. The two dogs ran around each other, sniffing and barking. Peggy loved playing with Princess! Despite her posh name, Princess was a lot of fun.

"Nice outfit," said Peggy.

"Trust me, it wasn't my idea," said

Princess, rolling on her back in the grass and getting her pink coat dirty.

Chloe beckoned Hannah over. "Come and see Daisy's babies!"

"When were they born?" Hannah asked.

"Four weeks ago," said Ellie. "Hey – speaking of birthdays, are you going to have a party this year, Chloe?"

Chloe shrugged. "Not sure. My parents haven't said anything about it."

As the girls cooed over the baby bunnies, Princess started chewing on a deckchair's seat cushion. "Aw," she said. "I used to have so much fun with my brothers and sisters."

Peggy had happy memories of playing with her siblings, too. *I wonder how they are all doing,* she thought.

"My sister Diva lives with a famous pop star now," boasted Princess through a mouthful of cushion foam. "I saw a picture of her in the newspaper – she was in the singer's handbag."

"Wow," said Peggy, impressed. She hoped her brother and sisters had all found forever homes as happy as hers. Peggy shuddered as she remembered her first owner, who hadn't been very kind. She had dumped Peggy at an animal shelter when she got bored of looking after her. But it had worked out for the best, because Chloe and her family had visited the shelter and adopted Peggy.

"You're so lucky," said Chloe. "Now you have six bunnies!"

"I'm only allowed to keep one of the babies," said Ellie. "We have to find new homes for the others. When they're eight weeks old, they can leave their mother."

"I'd love to have a pet bunny," said Hannah. "But there's no way my parents will let me get another pet. Princess is such a handful."

"Hey," said Princess, looking up from the cushion she had shredded. "What is she talking about?"

"No idea," said Peggy. Then, before her

friend could ruin another cushion, she said, "Hey – let's have a tug-of-war."

As she and Princess tussled over a gardening glove, Peggy heard Chloe say, "Maybe my parents will let me adopt one of the bunnies . . ."

"Uh oh, Peggy," teased Princess. "Sounds like you have some competition."

"Very funny," said Peggy. She and Chloe had a special bond – nothing would ever come between them. Peggy

glanced over at the baby rabbits. They looked so tiny and vulnerable. She hoped with all her heart that they would find families to love them as much as Chloe loved her.

That evening, Peggy lay on the floor beside Chloe as the family ate dinner.

Dad carried a large bowl of salad to the table. "The lettuce is from the garden," he announced proudly, placing a big serving of salad on everyone's plate.

Finn speared a piece of lettuce with his fork and pulled a face. "*Blurgh*. I'm not a fan of rabbit food."

"Ooh! That reminds me!" said Chloe. "Guess what? Today at Ellie's—"

But Dad hadn't finished going on about his garden. "My radishes are just starting to sprout and I'm going to plant courgettes when the weather warms up. We should have a bumper crop this year."

"Lovely!" exclaimed Mum. "I've got a great recipe for chocolate and courgette loaf. I can make some for the café."

"And Mummy is going to sell unicorn hot cross buns at the café too," said Ruby proudly.

Mum nodded. "They turned out surprisingly well."

Chloe tried again. "Ellie's pet bunny—"

"Ooh! Can I make some unicorn hot cross buns for the Easter bunny?" interrupted Ruby.

Chloe sighed in frustration.

Let her speak, thought Peggy.

"Go on, Chloe," said Mum, holding up her hand to silence the others.

"Ellie's pet bunny had babies," said Chloe, "but she's not allowed to keep them all. Can we adopt one?"

Mum and Dad exchanged looks.

Dad scratched his head. "I don't know," he said. "We're all pretty busy, what with work and school."

"And we've already got Peggy to look after," added Mum.

But I'm no trouble at all, thought Peggy.

"Please, please, please?" pleaded Chloe, clasping her hands together.

"Bunnies can't be that much work," said Finn. "You don't have to take them for walks."

"And the bunny can be Peggy's friend," said Ruby.

Chloe smiled at her brother and sister

gratefully. But Mum and Dad still didn't look convinced.

"It can be my birthday present," said Chloe. "If you let me get a bunny, I won't ask for anything else."

Wow, thought Peggy. I guess she really wants a bunny. She knew she had to help . . .

Peggy whined and pawed Mum's leg. "Go on, let Chloe get a bunny," she begged.

"See," said Chloe. "Peggy wants us to get a bunny."

Everyone laughed. Then Dad caught Mum's eye and they both shrugged.

"Oh, go on," said Dad, smiling. "I

suppose the more the merrier."

"Yes, you can get a bunny," said Mum. "But you'll need to look after it."

"Yay!" cried Chloe, giving each of her parents a hug. Then she picked up Peggy and gave her a cuddle, too.

"Guess what, Peggy," cried Chloe. "You won't be the only pet in the family much longer!"

That night, as they snuggled up together in bed, Chloe couldn't stop talking about the baby bunny. "I wish I didn't have to wait four whole weeks to take one home."

Peggy licked Chloe's nose. She was looking forward to the bunny's arrival, too.

"I'm going to adopt the little black and white one," said Chloe, stroking Peggy's back. "Ellie said she's the only girl in the litter." She sighed happily. "I fell in love with her the minute I saw her."

Soon, Chloe was snoring softly, a smile on her face. But Peggy couldn't fall asleep. Suddenly, she felt worried. She couldn't stop thinking about what Princess had said, about having competition.

Don't be silly, Peggy told herself. *Chloe loves you*.

But what if she loved the bunny more?

Chapter Three

Peggy didn't think that Chloe could get any more excited about the bunny's arrival, but she was wrong. Over the next few weeks, Chloe hardly talked about anything else. It was the first thing she told Peggy about when she got back from school.

"Ellie's found homes for all the babies," she announced one day.

"The bunnies tried radishes for the first time today," she reported a few days later.

Some days, Chloe went to visit the bunnies after school instead of coming straight home to play with Peggy the way she used to. Peggy missed spending time with her.

"I got to hold my bunny," Chloe told Peggy when she came home with a huge smile on her face. "You would not believe how soft her fur is."

I've got soft fur too, thought Peggy.

She was looking forward to the

weekend, when Chloe would finally be able to play with her. But on Saturday morning, Chloe had other ideas . . .

In the living room, Finn was sitting in front of the laptop wearing headphones. He nodded his head along to a rock video, drumming to the music with two pencils.

"Finn!" shouted Chloe, but he couldn't hear her. She lifted the headphones off her brother's ears.

"Hey!" he said.

"I need the computer," said Chloe. "I've got to research rabbit care because Ellie says I can take my bunny home soon."

"Tough. You'll just have to wait until

I'm done." Finn put his headphones back on.

"Not fair!" cried Ruby, who was building a LEGO castle on the floor. "I'm using the computer next. I want to play games."

"MUUUUM!" wailed Chloe, Ruby and Finn.

Peggy covered her ears with her paws.

Mum ran into the living room holding a kitchen timer. "Everyone calm down. You know you need to share the laptop. Finn, you've been staring at a screen long enough. Go and get some fresh air."

Huffing, Finn took his headphones off and stomped outside.

"My turn!" squealed Ruby.

"Not so fast, young lady," said Mum. "You need to do your homework first – then you can play games." She turned to Chloe and set the timer. "You can use the computer for half an hour, starting . . . now."

Chloe quickly slid into the seat and typed "rabbit care" into the browser. As Chloe read page after page of information, Peggy sat patiently next to her. This wasn't her idea of fun, but at least she was spending time with Chloe.

"Awww, bunnies are so cute," said Chloe, scrolling through pictures.

"Let me see," said Peggy. She jumped

up on to Chloe's lap. A picture of a lop-eared rabbit filled the screen. "Hi there!" Peggy barked. Resting her front paws on the keyboard, she sniffed the bunny, her nose leaving smudge marks on the screen.

BEEP! The screen went blank and then an error message appeared.

"Oh, Peggy," sighed Chloe. "You've crashed the computer."

I was just trying to be friendly, thought Peggy.

"Oh well," said Chloe. "My time was almost up anyway."

They went into the kitchen, where Mum was helping Ruby with her reading and Finn was pouring himself a glass of water.

"So what did you learn?" Mum asked Chloe.

"We need to buy a hutch for the bunny to live in," said Chloe.

"We don't need to buy one," said Finn. "I can build one."

"Really?" asked Chloe, looking doubtful.

"Sure," said Finn. "I learned how to do woodwork at school. And we've got plenty of wood in the garage."

"That's a wonderful idea," said Mum.

"I need to get a water bottle and a food bowl, too," said Chloe.

"What do bunnies eat?" asked Ruby.

"Mostly grass, hay and leafy greens," said Chloe. "And fruit and vegetables for a treat."

"Can I go and help Daddy in the garden?" Ruby asked Mum. "I'll tell him we need lots of leafy things for the bunny."

"Of course," said Mum. She closed Ruby's homework book and turned to Chloe. "You and I can go to the pet store and pick up some supplies."

Great idea! thought Peggy. The pet store was one of her favourite places. It had chewy toys, tasty treats and there were always lots of other animals to talk to. She grabbed her lead with her teeth and trotted over to Chloe.

"No, Peggy," said Chloe, hanging the lead back up. "You stay here."

Aww, thought Peggy. *Not fair!*

As she waited impatiently for Chloe to return, Peggy looked for someone to play with. The sound of banging was coming from the garage. Peggy peered inside and saw that Finn had made a start on the rabbit hutch.

"Don't come in here, Peggy," he said, hammering in a nail. "There are lots of sharp tools. I don't want you to get hurt."

Peggy wandered out to the garden, hoping that Ruby would play fetch.

"I can't play, Peggy," said Ruby, who was carefully putting seeds in the soil. "I'm helping Daddy."

When Chloe finally came home, Peggy pawed her leg eagerly. "Come on," she yipped. "Let's go out and play!"

"Sorry, Peggy," said Chloe, getting out her craft things. "I'm busy. I'm going to make some toys for the bunny with kitchen roll tubes."

I can't wait for the bunny to get here, thought Peggy, flopping down on the ground. *Then everything can go back to normal . . .*

The following weekend, Finn called everyone out to the garden. They gathered around a large object, covered with a cloth.

"Ta da!" Finn swept the cloth off, revealing the homemade rabbit hutch. It was a wooden box with four legs, a wire mesh window and a little door. Felt tiles covered the roof, to keep it snug and dry.

"Wow!" cried Chloe, clapping her hands. "It's amazing!"

"Well done, son," said Dad, putting his arm around Finn's shoulder.

Finn beamed with pride.

"Now we can get it ready!" said Chloe. She and Ruby lined the bottom of the hutch with straw, hung up a water bottle and set out the toys she'd made.

I'm bored, thought Peggy, sniffing around the garden. Her ears perked up as she heard a scrabbling noise coming from the other side of the fence. A moment later, a large, stripy ginger cat leaped down and stalked across the grass to her.

"What's going on here?" asked Tiger, his green eyes glinting mischievously. "Is

that cage for you, Pig Tail?"

"Chloe's getting a new bunny," Peggy explained to the cat who lived next door. "And my name isn't Pig Tail."

"Oh, so you're being replaced," sniffed Tiger. "Can't say I blame them."

"No!" said Peggy. "Don't be ridiculous. I'm not going anywhere."

"Sure, Pig Tail," drawled Tiger, sitting down and licking his paws. "You keep telling yourself that."

Peggy knew the mean old cat was just trying to upset her. Her friendship with Chloe was special.

So why did she feel so worried?

DING DONG! The next morning the doorbell rang. Peggy barked loudly, in case her family hadn't heard it.

"I'll get it!" shouted Chloe, running to open the door. Ellie stood on the doorstep, holding a carry case. Inside it was the black and white bunny!

"Bye bye, bunny," said Ellie, handing the case to Chloe and then waving goodbye.

The little rabbit's blue eyes blinked nervously as she peered through the bars of the carrier.

"Don't be scared," Peggy reassured her. "You'll like it here."

Out in the garden, Chloe eagerly lifted her new pet out of the carrier.

"I'm so glad you're finally here!" she said, giving the bunny a cuddle.

The bunny had grown since Peggy had last seen her, but she was still small enough to fit neatly in Chloe's hands.

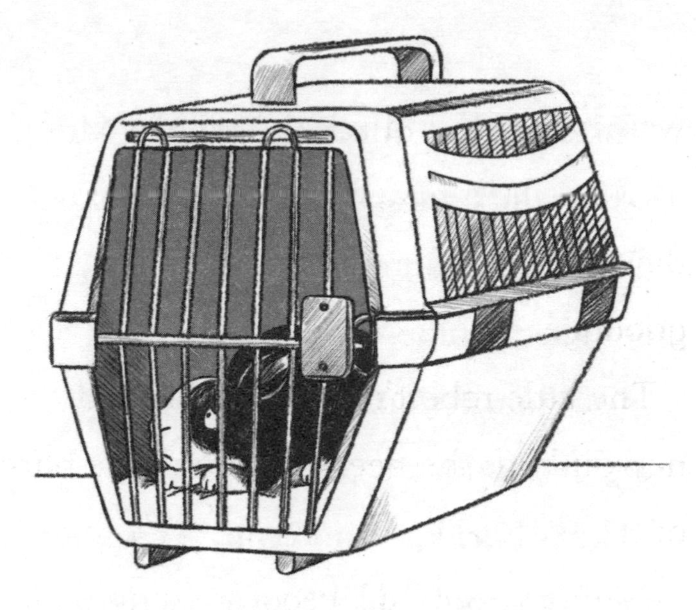

Peggy watched as Chloe rubbed her cheek against the bunny's fur.

"My turn! My turn!" clamoured Ruby.

Chloe placed the bunny carefully in her little sister's hands.

"She's so tiny," said Ruby. "She makes Peggy look huge."

Hey, thought Peggy. *I'm only little.*

"Oh, she's just adorable," sighed Mum, stroking the bunny's ears.

"What are you going to name her?" Dad asked Chloe.

"You should name her Patches," suggested Ruby.

"That's boring," said Finn. "How about something cool – like Storm or Rocket."

Chloe shook her head. "I'm going to call her Coco – because she's an Easter bunny."

"And the Easter bunny brings chocolate," said Ruby, passing the bunny back to Chloe.

"It's perfect," said Dad.

Peggy thought so too. "Hi, Coco!" she

barked, jumping up and down to try and get a better view of the bunny. "I'm Peggy."

The bunny didn't reply. She just trembled in Chloe's hands.

"Oh no! Coco's frightened," said Chloe. "Peggy's scaring her."

"I'd better take her inside," said Mum, scooping Peggy up.

"Noooo!" yelped Peggy, squirming. "I want to stay with all of you!"

But Mum put her inside the house and shut the door behind her. Peggy ran to the patio doors and peered out. She

watched sadly as her family fussed over the bunny. As Chloe stroked Coco, Dad offered the bunny a spinach leaf from the garden and Finn proudly demonstrated the hutch's features.

Tiger had been right, after all. Peggy's family weren't interested in her any more. Now all they cared about was the bunny. If Peggy wanted to keep their love, she'd have to be more like Coco.

Somehow, thought Peggy, *I'll just have to turn into a bunny.*

Chapter Four

If Peggy was going to become a bunny, she'd need to find out more about them. Luckily there was plenty of opportunity to watch Coco, since playing with her new pet was all Chloe wanted to do any more!

As Chloe got Coco out of her hutch

the next day, Peggy lay on the grass and kept her eyes on the bunny. Coco's nose twitched adorably as Chloe waved a long piece of grass in front of her. Peggy wriggled her nose, trying to copy the bunny.

"Come on," coaxed Chloe.

The bunny hesitated for a moment, then she hopped over to Chloe – *HOP! HOP! HOP!* – and nibbled the grass.

"Good girl!" said Chloe, picking up the bunny and giving her a cuddle.

Peggy looked down at the lawn doubtfully. If eating grass made Chloe happy, she'd just have to give it a try. Sighing, she bit off a big clump and chewed.

Yuck! It tasted terrible. She spat the grass out.

But it wasn't just the grass leaving

a bad taste in her mouth . . . Peggy swallowed hard as she stared at Chloe and Coco snuggling together.

"That's right," purred Tiger, slinking across the top of the garden fence. "A predator watches its prey and then—" he jumped down – "ATTACKS!" The cat nodded at Peggy approvingly. "You're not as stupid as you look."

"I'm not trying to attack the bunny," said Peggy, horrified. "I'm trying to become one."

"I take it back," said Tiger, shaking his head. "You *are* as stupid as you look." He began to preen, smoothing his whiskers. "Anyway, if you're going to become another animal, be a cat. We felines are the best." Tiger stretched, his fur shining like copper in the sunshine. "Elegant . . . independent . . . nimble . . ."

"Selfish . . ." added Peggy under her breath as Tiger sauntered away, ". . . lazy . . . rude."

"Chloe!" called Mum from the back door. "Don't forget to take Peggy for her morning walk."

Sighing, Chloe put Coco back in her hutch. "Come on, Peggy," she said, sounding annoyed. "Let's hop to it."

She used to love taking me for walks, thought Peggy as Chloe clipped on her lead.

But Chloe had given her a brilliant idea – she would hop to the park!

HOP – HOP – HOP – STOP!

Why was it so hard to get all four of her paws in the air at the same time? Coco could do it and she was only a baby.

HOP – HOP – HOP – HOP – STOP!

Peggy did a few more jumps then stopped to catch her breath. Hopping was much trickier than it looked. She glanced up at Chloe, hoping her friend would be impressed, but she hadn't even noticed. Concentrating hard, Peggy tried again.

HOP – HOP – HOP – HOP – FLOP!

She tripped and fell on her bottom. *OUCH!*

So that's why bunnies have fluffy tails, thought Peggy, *for bottom cushioning!*

"Hurry up, Peggy," said Chloe, tugging the lead. "We're never going to get to the park at this rate."

When they finally got to the park, Chloe spotted Hannah and Princess by the playground. She let Peggy off her lead, and ran over to join her friend.

Peggy decided to practise hopping again.

HOP – HOP – HOP! She slowly jumped across the grass, trying hard not to lose her balance. Princess ran over to her. Today she was wearing a tartan jacket and a matching bow. "You're limping!" Princess said. "Did you hurt your paw?"

"I'm not limping," explained Peggy. "I'm hopping. Look!"

HOP – HOP – HOP!

"You look ridiculous," said Princess.

"Dogs aren't supposed to hop. They run! And scamper! And frolic!" To prove her point, Princess ran around Peggy in circles, until she got dizzy and collapsed on the grass, panting.

"I don't want to be a dog any more," said Peggy. "I want to be a bunny."

Princess sat up and stared at her friend, astonished. "Say *whaaaat?* That's crazy talk! Why would anyone want to be a boring old bunny when they could be a dog? Intelligent, loyal, brave and – let's face it – absolutely gorgeous." She raised one leg in the air and scratched her ear. "That's why they call us 'man's best friend' of course."

Peggy sighed. "I used to be Chloe's best friend – but now she has Coco. She doesn't want to play with me any more."

"Well, I still like playing with you," said Princess. "So stop hopping and let's play!"

The two little dogs rolled on the grass, chased squirrels and barked at birds.

All too soon, Peggy heard Chloe

calling her name.

Peggy ran over to Chloe, who clipped on her lead and said, "Let's get back home – I want to check on Coco."

"See what I mean," Peggy said to Princess. "Coco, Coco, Coco! That's all Chloe's interested in now."

Peggy hopped down the path with Chloe, hoping she looked like a bunny.

"You're not fooling anyone," Princess called after her. "Bunnies don't have curly tails!"

When they got back home, Peggy flopped on the floor, panting. Hopping was exhausting! She decided to try something a bit less energetic.

Twitch! Twitch! Twitch! She wriggled her nose the way Coco did, hoping she looked as cute as the bunny.

AAAACCCHHOOOO!

Peggy tried once more, wriggling her nose in a bunny-like way. She sneezed again.

AAAACCCHHOOOO!

"Oh dear," said Mum. "I think Peggy has come down with a cold."

Chloe nodded. "That makes sense. She was acting strange on our walk." She patted Peggy on the head. "Poor Peggy."

"Let's keep her indoors so she can get some rest," said Mum.

"Honestly, I'm fine!" said Peggy, trying to follow Chloe outside.

"Stay inside, Peggy," said Chloe firmly. "You're not very well." She went into the garden, shutting the door behind her.

Mum filled up a hot water bottle, wrapped it in a towel and placed it next to Peggy on the sofa. "Poor little bunny," she said, stroking Peggy's back. *Hmm,* thought Peggy. *Mum called me a bunny.*

Maybe her plan was starting to work, after all!

After a boring day cooped up indoors,

Peggy was glad when it was bedtime. She was careful not to sneeze again, as she couldn't face the thought of another day stuck in the house. She wandered into Ruby's bedroom, where Chloe and her sister were choosing a book to read at bedtime.

"I want this one," said Ruby, taking a picture book about a dancing giraffe off the shelf.

"We had that one last night," said Chloe. "I want Dad to read a chapter from Harry Potter."

"That's too scary," said Ruby. "It will give me nightmares."

Trying to be helpful, Peggy pulled a

well-worn picture book about a dog off the shelf with her teeth. She wagged her tail hopefully.

"Looks like you're feeling better," said Chloe, taking the book out of Peggy's mouth.

But to Peggy's disappointment, Chloe slid the book back on the shelf. "How about this one?" she said, holding up a little white book instead. "We haven't read this for ages."

Dad came into the bedroom. "Have you chosen a book?" he asked.

Chloe handed him the little book and he smiled. "Ah, *The Tale of Peter Rabbit*. That's a classic. Good choice – it *is* almost Easter, after all."

"Yay!" said Ruby. "Soon the Easter bunny will bring us treats!"

Peggy sighed. *Bunnies* . . . There was no escaping them!

They all snuggled together on the bed and Dad began to read. To her surprise, Peggy found herself enjoying the story.

It was about a naughty rabbit named Peter who stole vegetables from Mr McGregor's garden. As she listened to the story, Peggy suddenly had an amazing idea.

I know how I can be more like a bunny! she thought happily.

Chapter Five

"Walkies, Peggy!" called Chloe the next morning.

Wagging her tail, Peggy ran to fetch her lead. She trotted along next to Chloe, not bothering to hop because she was too eager to get to the park. She couldn't wait to tell Princess her plan.

But Hannah and her dog weren't at the park. Peggy whined sadly.

"Sorry, Peggy," said Chloe. "Hannah's gone to visit her grandparents. And Ellie's family went to the seaside. The Easter holidays are going to be *soooo* boring – there's nobody around to play with."

I'm still here, thought Peggy.

Chloe watched two kids whizz past on their bikes. She sighed longingly. "I wish I had a new bike. But I told Mum and Dad that all I wanted for my birthday was a bunny."

Peggy wished that Chloe had asked for a bicycle instead. Then she would still like her best instead of Coco.

One of the boys popped a wheelie, while the other rang his bell.

"Let's go back home," said Chloe, turning around. "I'll remind Dad to fix the tyre on my old bike. It's too small, but it's better than nothing."

When they got home, Chloe and Peggy couldn't find Dad pottering in the garden. Cocking her ears, Peggy heard noises coming from the garage.

"Dad!" called Chloe, hurrying over.

But Finn came out of the garage instead. "You can't come in," Finn told his sister, wiping grease off his hands with a rag.

"Why not?" Chloe asked suspiciously.

"Dad and I are working on a project together," said Finn.

CLANG! Something metal hit the garage floor. *What's going on in there?* thought Peggy, trying to peek past Finn's legs.

"What are you making?" Chloe tried to peer around the door but Finn blocked the way.

"It's a father and son thing. Guys only."

"Won't be long, sweetie," called Dad from inside the garage.

"This is so unfair," huffed Chloe. "Girls can do anything boys can. MUM!!!"

Peggy trailed behind Chloe as she stomped into the kitchen. The table was completely covered in newspaper and a big bowl of glue.

"What are you doing?" asked Chloe.

"Oh!" gasped Mum, quickly grabbing a sheet of newspaper and holding it up to her face. "Just reading the newspaper."

Peggy cocked her head to the side. She was pretty sure the paper was upside down . . .

"Making an Easter bonnet!" blurted Ruby, wrapping a sheet of newspaper around her head.

"Can I make one too?" asked Chloe.

"NO!" shouted Mum and Ruby.

"Um, we don't have enough newspaper," said Mum apologetically.

That's odd, thought Peggy. There was enough newspaper on the table to open a newsagent's!

"Whatever," said Chloe, shrugging. She and Peggy went out to the garden. As they headed across the grass, Chloe grumbled, "Mum and Dad are always busy with Ruby and Finn. They probably don't even remember it's my birthday next week."

Chloe opened the hutch and took Coco out. "Good thing I have you to play with, Coco," said Chloe, rubbing noses with the bunny.

And me, thought Peggy, pawing her friend's leg.

"You can play too, Peggy," said Chloe. "But you need to be gentle." She set Coco down on the grass.

"Hi," said Peggy.

The bunny stared at her, quivering.

"You're lucky, Coco," said Chloe, stroking the rabbit's fluffy back. "You don't have to share your hutch with anyone."

But Peggy wondered whether Coco was missing her brothers. Maybe her hutch felt lonely without her four siblings to snuggle up with. Peggy had really missed her brothers and sisters when she first left them.

The poor little thing is probably homesick, she thought, remembering all the fun games she used to play with Pablo, Pippa and Polly.

"Hey, Coco," she said. "Want to play tug-of-war?"

"I-I don't know how," said the bunny so quietly Peggy could barely hear it.

"Well, how about hide-and-seek?" she suggested.

"I don't know that one either," whispered Coco.

"Chase?" Peggy tried again.

The bunny shook her head.

"It's easy and really fun," said Peggy. "I can teach you—" She batted the bunny with her paw and barked,

"Tag! You're it!"

"Naughty Peggy!" shouted Chloe. She scooped the bunny up protectively. "You mustn't hurt Coco."

"I was just playing," yelped Peggy.

Cuddling the bunny, Chloe marched indoors, leaving Peggy all alone.

Peggy moped around the garden, imagining all the fun Chloe and Coco were having together inside. *I've GOT to become a bunny,* she thought desperately. Chloe obviously wasn't interested in pugs any more.

When she came to Dad's vegetable patch, Peggy perked up. Here was her chance to be just like Peter Rabbit!

Hopping over the little border, Peggy

wandered down the neat rows of vegetables, her paws sinking into the soil. She sniffed at the fragrant herbs and giant rhubarb leaves, trying to decide where to begin.

Aha! she thought, spotting some lettuce. *Peter Rabbit loved lettuce!*

Peggy began to dig, her paws churning up the soil. She worked her way down the row, digging up every head of lettuce she could find.

"Pardon me!" she said to an earthworm as he wriggled away and disappeared back into the soil.

When Peggy had finished digging up all the lettuces, she hurried to the next

row and started on the radishes. Clumps of earth flew through the air as she dug out all the fat red bulbs.

But before she could move on to the onions, she heard—

"Peggy!"

She looked up and saw Dad sprinting across the garden.

"Look!" barked Peggy proudly, wagging her tail. "I'm just like Peter Rabbit!"

But as he got closer, Dad didn't look impressed. He looked furious!

"Bad dog!" shouted Dad. "What have you done to my vegetables?"

"I was trying to be like Peter Rabbit," explained Peggy, dropping a radish at his feet.

The rest of the family came running outside to see what had caused the commotion.

"Oh, dear," said Mum, putting her arm around Dad.

"I'm so sorry, Dad," said Chloe, lifting Peggy out of the vegetable patch. "I don't know what's got into Peggy all of a sudden."

Peggy was confused. Why was it cute when bunnies dug up the garden, but naughty when dogs did it?

"I think she's misbehaving because she's jealous of Coco," said Mum.

"We're going to have to do something about it," said Dad, gazing in dismay at his ruined vegetable patch.

Peggy's heart sank. She thought that acting like a bunny would please her family.

So why did they seem so angry at her?

Later that day, Peggy overheard Mum

and Dad whispering together. She strained her ears, but she could only catch bits of their conversation:

Don't tell Chloe . . .

We'll do it in the morning . . .

Oh no! thought Peggy. She suddenly realised what Mum and Dad were planning – they were going to take her back to the dog shelter!

Peggy moaned softly. She never wanted to go back to that horrible place. This was her home now!

She looked out of the window and saw Chloe putting hay in Coco's hutch. As she watched, her worry turned to anger.

This is all Coco's fault.

Her life had been perfect before the bunny had arrived. Peggy had been Chloe's special friend, before Coco came between them and ruined everything. There was only room for one pet in this family.

Well, Peggy wasn't going to go without a fight. She was done with trying to become a bunny. It was time for a new plan.

It's me or the bunny, she thought grimly. *Coco's got to go!*

Chapter Six

"It's Easter!!!!!" shrieked Ruby, bouncing on Chloe's bed. Peggy yawned and burrowed into Chloe. She was hoping for a lie-in, but Chloe scurried out of bed.

"Let's see what the Easter bunny has brought us!" she said, quickly pulling on some clothes.

"Hopefully lots of chocolate eggs in the garden!" cried Ruby.

Humph! thought Peggy, reluctantly waddling out of bed. As if Coco wasn't annoyingly perfect enough already, now she'd brought them all chocolate!

The girls ran downstairs and were about to run into the garden, but Mum stopped them. "Scrambled eggs before chocolate eggs."

"Awww," sulked Ruby. "But I want to have an Easter egg hunt."

"First eat your breakfast," said Dad, buttering a piece of toast for her.

"Anyway," said Finn, raising his eyebrow playfully, "who says the Easter bunny brought you anything?"

Ruby and Chloe looked worried until Mum chuckled and said, "Your brother's just teasing you. I'm sure I heard something hopping around the garden last night."

But Finn had given Peggy a brilliant idea. Suddenly, she knew how to make the oh-so-perfect little bunny look bad for a change!

The back door was slightly ajar, so Peggy slipped out into the garden. Dew sparkled on the grass and brightly coloured tulips swayed gently in the breeze. But the flowers weren't the only thing adding colour to the garden . . .

Underneath bushes and tucked inside flower pots, shiny foil wrappers twinkled in the sunshine.

Easter eggs!

"Happy Easter, Peggy," Coco called from her hutch.

Oh, so you're not scared of me now, thought Peggy. Coco had probably just been pretending to be frightened when Chloe was around to make Peggy look naughty!

Peggy didn't bother to reply. She wasn't interested in being friends now – not when Coco was forcing her out of her home!

Peggy started searching for chocolate

eggs. If she got rid of all of them, the children would think Coco hadn't brought them anything for Easter. Then it would be bye-bye bunny!

For a moment Peggy felt a twinge of guilt. But desperate times called for desperate measures. *It's Coco . . . or me.*

Peggy found an Easter egg hidden behind a watering can. She bit through the pink foil wrapper to get to the chocolate inside. Peggy gobbled it up and then found a shiny blue egg hidden underneath a rose bush. Nudging it out with her paw, she quickly ate that one too.

"There's one under the wheelbarrow,"

called Tiger, who was watching her from the top of the fence.

Peggy found eggs hidden in the flowerbeds and vegetable patch, inside a wooden trug and behind a garden gnome. There was even one tucked inside

a tulip, its purple wrapper blending in with the petals!

I don't know why Chloe likes this so much, thought Peggy, licking chocolate off her chops. It was sickly sweet and made her very thirsty. She lapped up some water dripping from the water butt. *Give me a sausage any day . . .*

But Peggy was a pug with a purpose! She ate every last Easter egg that she could find. Then she pushed the foil wrappers into a pile with her paws and buried them in the flowerbed to get rid of the evidence.

Ugh. Peggy groaned and flopped onto the grass. Her tummy felt funny. But at least all the Easter eggs were gone.

"Are you feeling OK?" asked Coco.

Like you care, thought Peggy.

Just then, the three children burst out of the house holding baskets.

"Woo hoo!" shouted Chloe. "I'm going

to find the most Easter eggs!"

"We'll see about that," said Finn.

"I should get a head start since I'm the littlest," said Ruby, darting forwards.

The children dashed around the garden, looking for chocolate eggs.

"They must be really well hidden," said Chloe, searching among the tulips on her hands and knees.

"I can't find any!" said Ruby, showing the others her empty basket.

"Me either," said Finn, scratching his head.

"Look what I found!" cried Chloe, beckoning her brother and sister over to the flowerbed. A bit of blue foil was sticking up from the soil. Chloe brushed the dirt away and found the stash of Easter egg wrappers.

Uh oh, thought Peggy.

"Someone ate all of our Easter eggs!" wailed Ruby.

Now Peggy was starting to feel bad. And it wasn't just because of the disappointed looks on the children's faces. Her tummy was really hurting!

She staggered to her feet and—*BLURGH!* – threw up a puddle of brown on to the grass.

"Peggy!" cried Chloe, running over to her.

"What's wrong with her?" asked Ruby,

her eyes filled with concern.

"Mum! Dad!" yelled Finn. "Come quick!"

"Oh dear," said Mum, hurrying into the garden. "Peggy must have eaten the Easter eggs."

Chloe's face turned pale. "Oh no! Chocolate is really bad for dogs, isn't it?"

Dad nodded, his face grim. "It's poisonous for them. We need to get Peggy to the vet right away."

As Dad drove to the vet, Chloe cradled Peggy in the back seat. "I'm sorry," she whispered, stroking her head. "I should have been paying more attention. I shouldn't have let you go outside when there was chocolate out there."

Peggy wanted to tell Chloe that it was OK, it wasn't her fault, but she felt dreadful. She lay limply in Chloe's arms, too weak to lift her head.

At the vet's surgery, they were rushed straight into an examination room. The vet, Dr Shah, put on a pair of gloves and placed Peggy on the cold, metal examining table. She checked her heart rate, took her temperature and listened to her breathing.

"It's a good thing you brought her in so quickly," she said. "Chocolate poisoning can be fatal to dogs. How much did she eat?"

"A lot," said Dad, biting his lip as Chloe clutched his hand anxiously.

The vet gave Peggy some medicine. "This will make her vomit – so it will bring up the chocolate."

Yuck, thought Peggy, forcing down the medicine. It tasted even worse than chocolate.

Suddenly, she felt queasy. She whimpered and then – *BLURGH!* – threw up again and again.

"Is Peggy going to be OK?" asked Chloe, her voice trembling.

"It's too soon to tell now," said the vet. "We'll keep her in overnight, so we can monitor her and get her re-hydrated."

"Can I stay with her?" asked Chloe.

"I'm afraid not," said Dr Shah. "But she'll be very comfortable in our animal hospital."

Tears rolled down Chloe's cheeks.

"Don't worry, sweetheart," said Dad, giving her a hug. "The vets will take good care of Peggy."

"You can come visit her in the morning," said Dr Shah. "Hopefully she'll be feeling much better by then."

"Goodbye, Peggy," said Chloe, gently stroking her back. "I love you so much. I can't bear the thought of anything bad happening to you."

I love you too, thought Peggy. She wished she could comfort her friend and lick her tears away, but she was much too ill.

"All I want for my birthday is for you to get better," whispered Chloe.

Then she was gone. And Peggy was all alone.

Chapter Seven

Peggy whimpered softly as the vet pricked her leg with a needle and attached an IV drip. Nearby, a bag of clear liquid hung from a metal stand.

"This is medicine to help you to get better," Dr Shah said, wrapping gauze around her leg to keep the IV in place.

When the vet had finished, a nurse in blue scrubs wheeled Peggy on a trolley into the overnight ward. She set Peggy down gently in a kennel lined with a fleece blanket and parked the IV drip stand just outside of it. Patting Peggy on the head, the nurse said, "Get some rest, sweetie. I'll be back to check on you soon."

Peggy's eyes began to feel very heavy and soon she was fast asleep.

Hours later, Peggy woke with a start in the middle of the night. *Where am I?* she thought, her heart racing. She looked around in alarm. There were metal bars in front of her. She was in a cage!

Pressing her face against the bars, she could see a row of other cages, filled with sleeping dogs.

I'm back at the dog shelter!

Peggy's worst nightmare had come true. "Get me out of here!" she howled. "I want to go home!"

"Hush," said a cocker spaniel in the cage next to her. "If you keep howling you'll wake everyone up."

"But I don't want to be back at the dog shelter," wailed Peggy.

This was exactly what she'd been trying to avoid by eating the chocolate!

"You're not at a dog shelter," said the spaniel, who had a bandaged paw. Her collar had a tag that said Mabel on it. "You're in the hospital. I'm not sure what's wrong with you – but you're definitely going to get a sore throat if you don't stop that howling."

"She's already given me a headache," said a gruff voice from the cage on the other side of Peggy.

It all came flooding back to Peggy – Coco . . . the Easter egg hunt . . . the chocolate . . . "I'm such a silly dog," she moaned, hiding her face with her paws. The medicine had made her tummy feel better, but she still felt sick when she realised how foolishly she had behaved.

"Silly dog! Silly dog!" squawked a parrot from the other end of the room.

"It's not your fault you got ill," said Mabel, sticking her good front paw through the bars to comfort Peggy.

"Yes it is," said Peggy. "I ate a bunch of chocolate eggs because I wanted to make my friend Chloe's new pet bunny look bad – but instead I made myself really sick."

"That does sound a bit silly," said the

gruff voice. Peggy looked over and saw a collie with a plastic cone around his neck.

"Seamus, that's not helping," said Mabel.

"He's right," said Peggy, sniffling. "I ruined Easter for Chloe and her family."

"You love them very much, don't you," said Mabel, resting her head on her paws thoughtfully.

"I do," said Peggy, her voice catching. "They adopted me from a dog shelter and I was scared they were going to take me back there."

"What made you think that?" asked Mabel.

"Because Chloe has a cute baby bunny for a pet now," said Peggy sadly. "She doesn't need me any more. All she wants to do is play with Coco."

Mabel thought for a moment, her head cocked to the side. "Hmmm," she said eventually. "Does Chloe have any brothers and sisters?"

Peggy nodded, her heart swelling with love as she thought about the children. "There's Finn – he tries to act like a tough rock star, but really he's a big softie. And little Ruby, who loves to play games and always shares her treats with me."

"So there are three children in your

family," said Mabel.

Peggy nodded. She wasn't sure what Mabel was getting at.

"Do their parents only love one of them?"

"Of course not!" said Peggy. "Mum and Dad love them all."

"You see," said Mabel, wagging her

tail. "Love isn't something that runs out. There's always enough to go around."

"She's right," purred a cat from the opposite side of the room. "I've just had a litter of six – but I love each one of my babies equally." She gazed down proudly at the tiny kittens nestled against her. "They are all precious to me."

"Congratulations," said Peggy. "Your babies are beautiful." She thought back to her own mum. She'd had her paws full with Peggy, Pablo, Paddy, Pippa and Polly – but she'd always made each puppy feel special and loved.

But Peggy still wasn't convinced. Mothers had to love their babies. But surely it was different for pets and their owners? "I used to be Chloe's special friend, but now all she seems to care about is Coco."

"It sounds to me like you're feeling jealous," said Mabel.

"I live on a sheep farm," said Seamus. "I love Farmer James and I know he loves me. But he has lots of other animals to care for too." The sheepdog turned around a few times to get comfortable, then settled down again on his blanket.

"Don't you find it hard to share him with all the others?" asked Peggy.

"When I was just a pup I felt jealous sometimes. I couldn't understand why Farmer James couldn't play with me, if one of the sheep needed his help. But soon I realised that Farmer James has to give his love to whoever needs it most – like when I hurt my leg out in the field. And at the end of the day, it's me curled up by his fire at night."

Peggy thought about how she got to sleep with Chloe in her cosy bed while Coco had to sleep outside, with nobody to snuggle up with.

"Maybe your friend Chloe is giving Coco a lot of attention right now because she's still settling in to her new home," suggested Mabel.

Peggy thought about how timid and nervous the bunny was. Peggy was used to her home, so she couldn't imagine anyone finding it scary. But maybe Coco was finding it hard to adjust. She needed Chloe – the way Peggy had needed her when she first came to live with her family.

"I guess I didn't think about it that way," admitted Peggy.

"Besides, it can be fun to have other animals around to talk to," said Seamus. "My friend Lulu is a llama."

Peggy sighed. "At least llamas are interesting. Bunnies are so . . . boring."

"Hey," said a voice from across the room. "Who are you calling boring?"

Peggy looked over and saw that the voice belonged to an enormous brown rabbit with a patch over one eye.

"Sorry," said Peggy.

"Silly dog!" squawked the parrot.

"I'll have you know that just because we bunnies are fluffy and talk quietly, it doesn't mean we aren't interesting," said the rabbit indignantly.

"Yeah, you shouldn't judge other creatures based on their appearance," said a Chihuahua. "I might look little and cute, but watch out—" He bared his sharp teeth and growled.

Yikes! Peggy made a mental note to steer clear of Chihuahuas.

Mabel nodded. "Coco might just be shy. She's probably very nice when you get to know her."

"I tried to play with her," said Peggy,

"but she doesn't even know any games."

"Then you'll just have to teach her," said Mabel. "Be like a big sister to her."

Peggy thought of how Finn and Chloe had taught their little sister Ruby how to do lots of things – from riding a scooter and skipping rope, to tying shoelaces and telling jokes. Maybe the other dogs were right – Coco needed a big sister to teach her things.

I really haven't given Coco a chance, thought Peggy guiltily. She'd been so worried about Coco replacing her, that she hadn't given much thought to how Coco was feeling.

Peggy knew how lucky she was. If Dad

hadn't got her to the vet in time, she could have died. She remembered the worry on Chloe's face as she'd held her tight.

I should never have doubted how much Chloe loves me, thought Peggy.

She'd been given a second chance – and she wasn't going to waste it.

When I'm well enough to go home, I'm going to make it up to Coco, thought Peggy. *I'll be the best big sister any bunny has ever had!*

Chapter Eight

"There she is!"

Looking up, Peggy saw Chloe and the rest of her family, followed by Dr Shah, coming into the overnight ward.

Peggy scrambled to her feet and barked joyfully, pawing the bars of her cage and wagging her tail. She had never been so happy to see anyone!

"Peggy!" said Chloe. She stuck her hand between the bars and tickled Peggy behind her ears. "I've been so worried about you."

"Me too," said Ruby. She crowded around Peggy's cage next to her sister.

"Me three," said Finn, grinning sheepishly.

"Oh, your family is so lovely," said Mabel, watching from the next cage.

"It really is!" said Peggy proudly.

"How's she doing?" Mum asked the vet.

Dr Shah looked at Peggy's chart and nodded. "I checked her over this morning, and she's doing much better."

"So Peggy's going to be OK?" asked Chloe.

The vet smiled. "You can take her home."

"Hurrah!" cheered Chloe, Ruby and Finn.

WOOF! WOOF! WOOF! barked Peggy happily.

"I'm glad you're going home. All this racket is giving me earache," grumbled Seamus. But Peggy could tell that the gruff sheepdog was pleased for her.

Dr Shah took Peggy out of her cage and gave her to Chloe. "Now don't eat any more chocolate, Peggy," she joked.

No chance, thought Peggy. She never wanted to touch chocolate again!

"Goodbye, Peggy," said Mabel.

"Bye," Peggy told the spaniel. "I hope you all get better soon."

"Don't forget what I told you – there's

always enough love to go around,"
Mabel reminded her. "It isn't something
that runs out."

"I won't forget," promised Peggy.
Safe in Chloe's arms, surrounded by
her whole family, she felt like her heart

might burst from all the love in it.

Back at home, Peggy wanted to go straight outside and apologise to Coco, but Chloe said, "No, Peggy. Dr Shah said you needed to take it easy."

For the rest of the day, everyone made Peggy feel special.

Finn sang her his new song.

Ruby gave her a cuddly toy to chew.

Dad cooked her sausages for dinner.

Mum held Peggy on her lap while they all watched television in the evening.

And at night, Peggy snuggled up with

Chloe in her soft, warm bed.

Peggy loved all of the treats and attention, but something was bothering her. She couldn't stop thinking about Coco, outside in her rabbit hutch.

I've got to make things right with Coco, Peggy thought before she drifted off to sleep.

The next day, she finally had her chance.

"I could really use everyone's help in the garden today," Dad announced at breakfast. "I want it to look good for next weekend."

"Why?" asked Chloe. "What's happening next weekend?"

Mum shot Dad a warning look. "Er, no particular reason," he said quickly. "It would just be good to get stuff done today while the weather's nice."

"Didn't you say the peas were ready to harvest," said Mum.

"Yes, that's right," said Dad. "And we need to plant the strawberries."

"Yum!" said Chloe. "I love strawberries."

"Mmm," said Finn. "Strawberry cheesecake . . ."

"Ooh, Mummy!" said Ruby. "Maybe we should make a cheesecake for the—"

"These dishes won't do themselves," Mum said, interrupting Ruby. She started noisily gathering up the breakfast things.

Peggy noticed Finn put his finger to his lips and wink at Ruby. *That's weird,* thought Peggy.

"Nobody even remembers it's my birthday next weekend," Chloe said to Peggy as they went out to the garden. "Oh, well. You're back at home – that's only thing that matters."

But Peggy could tell that Chloe was a bit disappointed. She decided to surprise her with some extra-slobbery licks as a birthday treat. She'd even give her friend her favourite chew toy, which was shaped like a turkey drumstick. Who wouldn't love that?

Chloe took Coco out of her hutch and placed her on the grass. Then she filled up a watering can from the water butt and went over to help the rest of the family in the vegetable patch.

"Peggy!" said Coco, hopping over to her. "I'm so glad you're feeling better. I was really worried when I heard you were ill."

"It was all my fault," said Peggy. "I did something really silly because I was jealous of you."

"What? If anything, it's me who

should be jealous," said Coco. "Chloe loves you so much. She takes you on walks, lets you sleep in her bed and she never stops talking about you."

Peggy glanced over and saw Finn, Chloe and Ruby working alongside their parents in the vegetable patch.

"Good job, Rubes," said Dad as Ruby planted a strawberry seedling in the soil.

"Thanks, hon," called Mum, as Finn lugged a bag of compost over from the shed. Then she kissed Chloe, who was weeding the vegetable patch next to her, on the top of her head.

The three children were very different, but their parents loved them all the same.

"Chloe loves both of us equally," said Peggy. "There's always enough love to go around in a family."

"You are so clever, Peggy," said Coco. The bunny's eyes gazed up at Peggy, shining with admiration. "I wish I knew as much as you do."

"Don't worry," said Peggy, "I'll teach you everything I know. There are lots of games we can play together."

"Really?" asked Coco, her whiskers trembling. "You'd do that?"

Peggy looked over at the vegetable patch again. Now Chloe was teaching Ruby how to water the plants, helping her hold the heavy watering can. "Of course," she said. "That's what big sisters are for."

"I've always wanted a sister," said Coco happily. "All the other bunnies in my litter were boys."

HISSSSS!

Peggy turned and saw Tiger watching them. He jumped down from the fence and landed neatly on all four paws. "Well, well, well, isn't this a touching scene," he said, his tail twitching from side to side.

Coco began to quiver with fear as the big cat stalked towards them.

"Go away, Tiger," said Peggy. "You're scaring Coco."

Tiger arched his back and bared his teeth. His fur stood on end, making him look even bigger and scarier. "What do you care, Pig Tail?" he sneered. "I'm doing you a favour. I thought you wanted to get rid of the bunny."

"Not any more!" said Peggy. "I like Coco now."

"Too bad," laughed Tiger. "I don't." *MEOWWWW!* He swiped his paw at the bunny.

Peggy leapt in front of Coco, Tiger's sharp claws barely missing her nose. "Nobody hurts my sister!" she growled. Peggy lunged forward, barking at the top of her lungs, and chased the big cat across the garden.

Yowling, Tiger scrambled over the fence, and into the safety of his own garden.

"That's right," Peggy barked. "And don't come back, you big scaredy-cat!"

"Oh no!" cried Chloe, dropping her watering can and running across the garden.

By the time she reached them, Peggy was curled up around Coco protectively.

"You're safe now," Peggy told her, nuzzling the bunny's tiny pink nose with her own flat brown one. Gradually, Coco's trembling stopped.

"Good girl, Peggy," said Chloe, stroking her back. "You saved Coco from that mean old cat."

Coco gazed up at Peggy adoringly. "That was so brave," she said. "You're my hero, Peggy!"

"*WOOF!*" barked Peggy happily. *I think I'm going to like being a big sister!*

Epilogue

The following Sunday, Peggy woke Chloe up on by covering her face with slobbery kisses. "Happy Birthday!" she barked.

But nobody else in the family remembered. They acted like it was just any other day.

"Don't forget to take Peggy for a walk," called Mum, as she headed out to the garden holding a cardboard box.

"I can't believe nobody even wished me happy birthday," Chloe said glumly as she and Peggy trudged around the park.

When they came back home, the house was empty.

"Hello?" called Chloe. She slid the patio doors open and—

"Surprise!"

Chloe gasped in astonishment. Peggy couldn't believe her eyes – the garden was filled with Chloe's friends! Pretty bunting hung from the fence, the table heaved with presents and balloons were tied to the back of every chair.

Mum and Dad wheeled a shiny new bike over to Chloe. "Happy Birthday, sweetheart," said Dad.

"I thought you forgot," said Chloe.

"As if we would forget your birthday,"

laughed Mum, giving Chloe a hug.

Ruby danced around her sister singing, "We tricked you! We tricked you!"

"How did you keep it a secret?" asked Chloe, beaming.

"You almost caught us out a few times," said Finn.

Dad nodded. "You almost walked into the garage when Finn and I were assembling your new bike."

"And Ruby and I had to pretend we were making Easter bonnets when we were actually making a piñata," chuckled Mum. She pointed to the donkey-shaped piñata hanging from an apple tree.

"So this is why you wanted the garden to look good," said Chloe.

"Busted!" said Dad, grinning.

As the children played party games, Peggy wandered over to Coco's hutch.

"What's going on?" asked Coco.

"It's a birthday party," explained Peggy. "It's something humans do to celebrate the day they were born. Chloe is ten – that's makes her an old lady in dog years."

"Come on everyone," called Mum. "Let's play Pin-the-Tail-on-the-Pug!"

"You'd better hide, Peggy," said Coco, looking worried.

"Don't worry," laughed Peggy. "It's just

a silly party game."

As blindfolded children tried to stick a curly tail on a big photo of Peggy, Chloe brought Ellie over to see Coco.

"Oh, she's grown so much in just a few weeks!" said Ellie. "How's she doing?"

"She's great," said Chloe. "As you can see, she and Peggy are the best of friends now."

"Just like us," said Ellie, putting her arm around Chloe.

A while later, Mum brought out a chocolate birthday cake topped with ten candles.

Everyone sang *Happy Birthday* to Chloe. As she blew out the candles, someone called, "Make a wish!"

"I don't need to," said Chloe, grinning. "My birthday wish has already come true – I've got two amazing pets."

She cut up the chocolate cake and handed slices out to her guests. "None for you, Peggy," she said, smiling.

But Peggy didn't mind one bit. She'd had enough chocolate to last her a lifetime. And nothing was sweeter than knowing her family loved her as much as she loved them!

The End

Have you read Peggy the pug's first adventure yet?

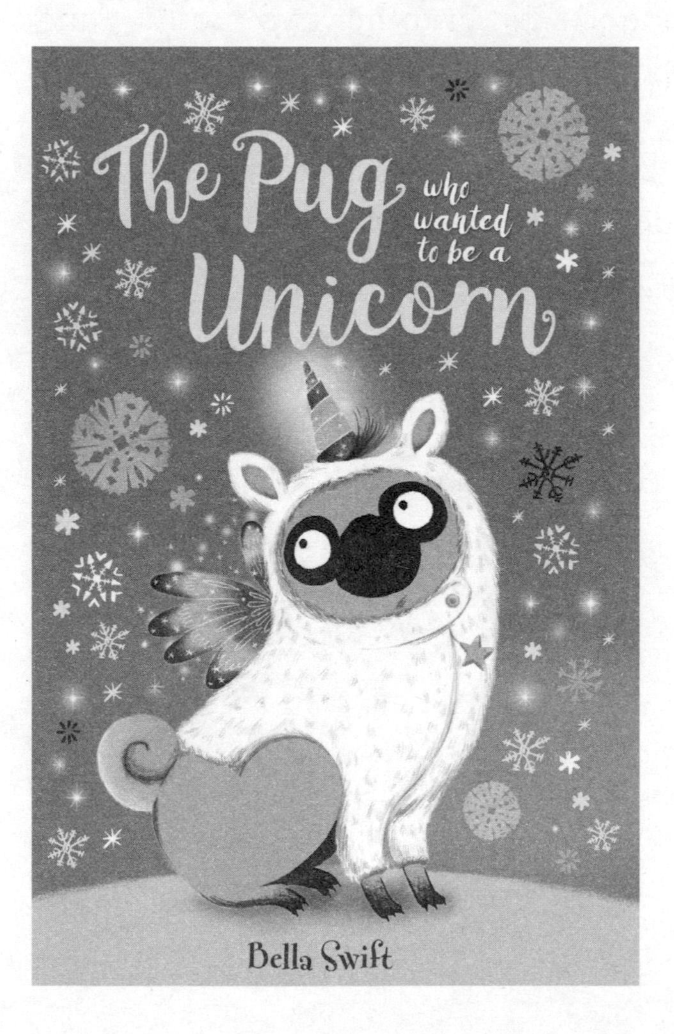

Peggy wriggled her little bottom and snuggled closer to her two brothers and two sisters. The five little pug puppies were curled up against their mother's side, snoozing in a furry heap of paws and curly tails. Sighing dreamily, Peggy nuzzled her squashed black nose against her mum's soft, tan-coloured fur.

Suddenly, her mum stood up, nudging the dozing puppies awake with her nose.

"Hey!" yelped Peggy's brother Pablo. "I was sleeping."

Yawning, the puppies clambered to their feet.

"Today's a very important day for all of you," announced their mum, gazing down at the puppies fondly with big brown eyes. "You're going home."

"Aren't we already home?" asked Peggy, puzzled.

"You're twelve weeks old now," her mum said gently. "So your new owners are coming today. They are taking you to your forever homes."

Peggy stared at her mum in confusion, her wrinkled forehead creasing even more. *Forever home? What's that?*

"Don't worry, little ones," the puppies' mum reassured them. "For every dog, there is a perfect owner. I know you will all find yours and be happy in your forever homes."

SLURP! SLURP! SLURP!

A rough pink tongue licked Peggy's face clean.

"Muuuuum!" protested Peggy, trying to squirm away from her mother's sloppy kisses.

"Don't wriggle," said her mother. "I want you to look your best." With one final slurp, she moved on to wash Peggy's sister Polly.

When all the puppies' fur was clean, their mum looked at them proudly. "There! Now you're ready to meet your new owners."

"I hope my owner has a big garden," yipped Peggy's brother Paddy, panting with excitement.

"I hope my owner gives me lots of tasty treats," yapped Pippa, the greediest puppy of the litter.

"I hope my owner likes to take naps," said Pablo, yawning. He stretched out his front paws, sticking his bottom in the air.

"What about you, Peggy?" asked her mum gently. "What type of owner do you want?"

Peggy thought for a moment. A garden would be nice. So would tasty snacks.

But that wasn't what Peggy wanted most of all. At last she said, "I hope my owner loves me."

Peggy's mum gazed at her puppies

tenderly, her eyes shining with affection. "'That's what I want for all of you, my dears.'"

Read The Pug Who Wanted to Be a Unicorn
to find out what happens next . . .

Have you read all these great animal stories by Bella Swift?

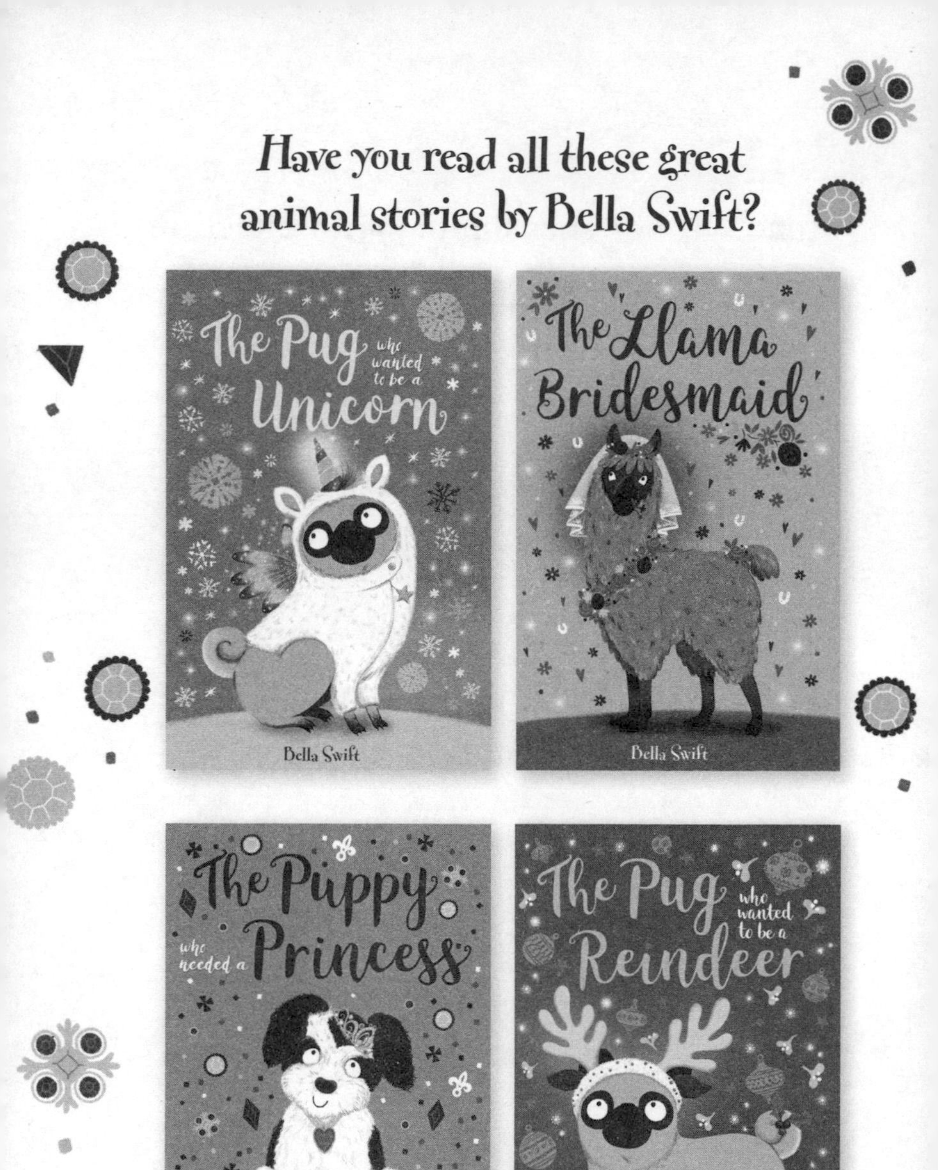